D1001003

The People Could Fly

AN AFRICAN-AMERICAN FOLKTALE

Retold by Ann Malaspina • Illustrated by Sole Otero

Published by The Child's World®
1980 Lookout Drive • Mankato, MN 56003-1705
800-599-READ • www.childsworld.com

Acknowledgments
The Child's World®: Mary Berendes, Publishing Director
Red Line Editorial: Editorial direction and production
The Design Lab: Design

ISBN 978-1623236175
LCCN 2013931390

Printed in the United States of America
Mankato, MN
July, 2013
PA02167

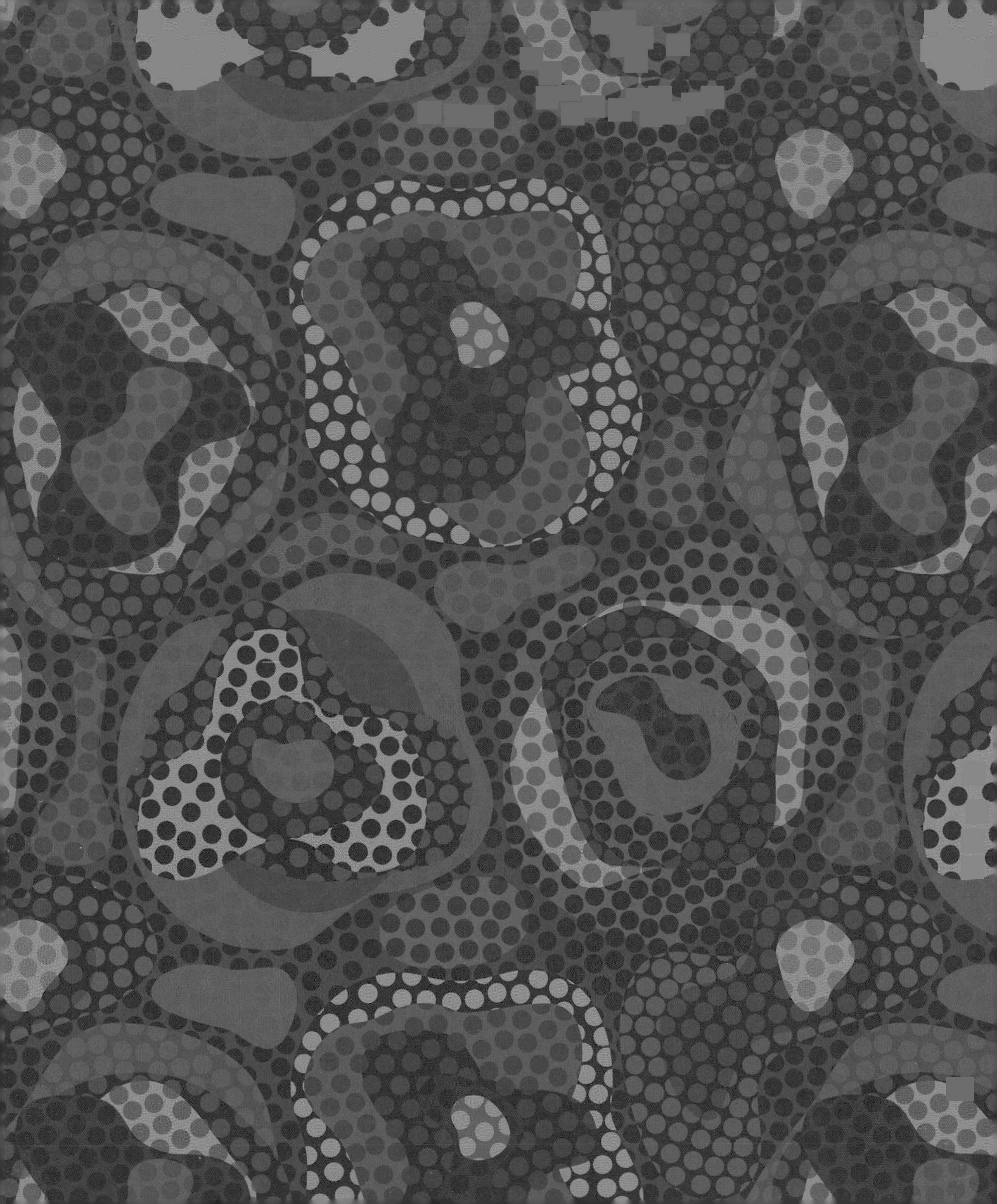

Not so long ago, people in Africa were sold into slavery. They were brought in chains to the Sea Islands, where they were put to work on cotton plantations. During planting season, under a brutal sun, slaves stamped barefoot down the rows, cutting away old roots and dropping seeds in the furrows. *Stamp. Cut. Drop. Stamp. Cut. Drop.*

One day, the master was anxious for the planting in his field to be done. In the field was a slave named Mariama, who carried a babe on her back. She was quicker than most, but when the babe cried, the overseer would shout at her from atop his horse. And when Mariama stopped to feed her babe, the overseer sent the driver to crack her with his long whip.

SLAP. SLAP. SLAP.

The babe cried even louder as her mother was struck. But afterward, Mariama continued her work.

Stamp. Cut. Drop. Stamp. Cut. Drop.

At sundown, the workday was over. The sea wind picked up as Mariama

walked to her cabin. Her old gran used to say that the salty wind blew all the way from Africa, where the yams are sweet as sugar and the sunlight pours down like rivers of gold.

As many of the older slaves did, Mariama's gran used to tell stories about Africa. Some of her stories were terrible. She would tell about the slave traders who tore her from her mother's arms and dragged her onto a ship. The ship voyaged across the sea. During the long journey, many of the African people that were packed in the holds down below died of starvation and illness.

Mariama closed her eyes, hearing her gran's voice again. She remembered another story. This one was not terrible at all. Back home in Africa, Gran had said, there were people who could fly.

"People don't have wings," Mariama would say, thinking about the birds pecking in the field and the mosquitoes buzzing in her ears.

Gran never seemed to hear but went on with her story. She said some of the people left their wings in Africa when they were forced onto the boat. Others hid their wings, waiting for the day when they could fly again.

"Fly away to freedom," Gran would say, laying her hand on Mariama's head.

Now Mariama's shoulders stung from the driver's whip. Her babe fussed and whimpered in her arms. All night long, she lay awake, wondering.

What if it were true?

What if she had wings to lift her to freedom?

Soon, tender shoots of cotton broke through the ground. The babe grew heavier. Mariama's back ached when she swung the hoe.

One day, Mariama noticed an old man bent over, working the next row.

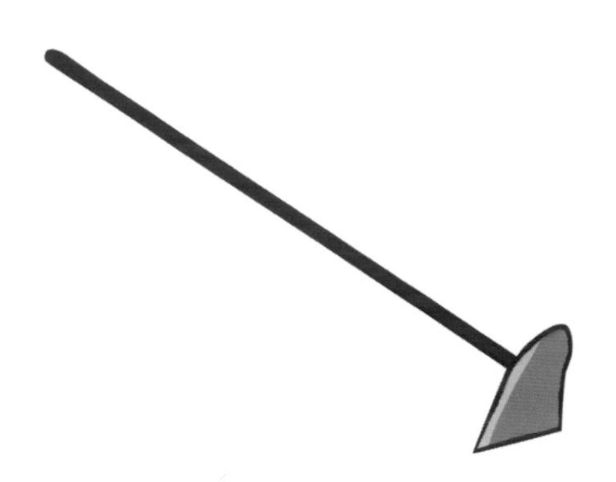

He was the root man who cured people when sickness came. The root man hoed the soil, chopping and pulling weeds.

Hoe. Chop. Pull. Hoe. Chop. Pull.

Though his arms were as knotty as pine branches, his breath was as thin as air in winter. Mariama said, "You need to rest, old man."

He shook his head, lifting his hoe again. The overseer watched from his horse, eyes squinting in the sun. When Mariama's babe cried from hunger, the root man told stories that distracted and quieted the infant, to keep from drawing the attention of the driver. Stories about Africa, sweet yams, and people with wings. Stories like her gran's.

"I saw those people fly with my own eyes," said the root man. "When they got sold into slavery, they hid away their wings. One day they gonna fly again."

He put his hand on the babe's tender head. "Fly away to freedom," he said.

Pain tore through Mariama's chest. It was the pain of wanting something so badly it felt like it could almost kill you.

"Tell me more!" she begged. And so the man continued.

"Quiet, old man!" The driver's horse threw mud in the air. The long whip cracked.

SLAP. SLAP. SLAP.

The root man did not utter a sound.

Afterward, Mariama brought him fresh water to drink. "Tell me more," she begged again.

The root man lifted his hoe and began to work in silence. He had said all he was going to say.

The blooms in the fields soon turned to hard green bolls. When autumn came, the bolls burst open. The cotton was ready. Sacks slung on their backs, the slaves picked the locks of cotton from the sharp hulls with their bare hands. At the same time, storms blew in from the sea. Rain poured down day after day. Mariama was afraid her babe would get sick in the downpour. But she had no choice but to wrap her babe and go to the field, where the workers were bent down and working, their hands bloody and sore. Her feet sank in the mud. The babe wailed, and Mariama's salty tears mingled with the rain.

The root man in the next row saw Mariama crying. He came over and leaned close, whispering strange words in her ear.

The words were familiar. They were magic words like her old gran used to say.

Mariama lay down her sack. She began walking to the sea, the babe in her arms.

“Where you going, girl?” the overseer’s voice called out. Hooves stamped and the whip cracked, but Mariama did not turn around.

The pain in her chest let go, and the rain stopped. Mariama closed her eyes, listening.

She heard her gran's voice in her head, telling her about Africa, the sweet yams, and the golden sun.

Fly away to freedom, her gran said.

She heard the root man's strange words.

Mariama grew as light as her babe's soft breath. Her feet rose off the ground. She felt as though she had wings lifting her like sails in the wind.

She flew above the overseer's horse and driver's whip, over the slave cabins and mucky fields. She flew over the Sea Islands and the shores where slavery dug its cruel heels. Clouds broke open, and the sunlight streamed down like the rivers of gold from her gran's stories.

The people toiling in the field saw what looked like a large black bird in the sky. “What is it?” they cried, pointing.

The root man told them to come near. Gathering round, they listened to his strange, magic words.

One by one, the people rose up. Their feet lifted off the ground, and wind pushed open invisible wings. The people who could fly passed over the plantation house, the muddy fields, the suffering and despair. Up, up, up they flew, like a flock of crows on their journey home.

“Fly away to freedom,” the root man whispered.

And so they did.

Southern United States
Sea Islands

Folktales about people in Africa who could fly were told by slaves in the Sea Islands of South Carolina and Georgia before the U.S. Civil War. Brought in chains from West Africa, they had been sold to American planters. The slaves were forced into hard labor on indigo, cotton, and rice plantations.

On cotton plantations across the South, slaves planted the seeds, chopped the weeds, and picked the cotton. After the cotton dried, the slaves ginned, or removed, the seeds by hand. Then they packed the cotton in bales to be sent to the mills. A burning sun, mosquitoes, and long hours of unpaid labor made the slaves' lives hard to endure.

Torn from their homelands and forbidden to learn to read or write, slaves often used oral, or spoken, storytelling to express their fears, hopes, and dreams. They told many stories about yearning for freedom. With the help of magic, people changed shape to escape their hard lives. The story you just read is one example. What do you think the invisible wings and flying in the story represent? What do you think happened to the people who flew away from the fields?

After slavery was abolished in 1865, many former slaves continued to live on the Sea Islands. Their descendants preserved their African heritage. For years they shared stories orally about people who could fly. These people were interviewed and their stories published in 1940 in the book *Drums and Shadows*. Since then, tales of people who can fly have spread far and wide.

ABOUT THE ILLUSTRATOR

Sole Otero is an illustrator from Buenos Aires, Argentina. She has a textile design degree and also works as a teacher.